Have You
Ever Ever Ever?

Colin McNaughton

Illustrated by Emma Chichester Clark

Have you ever, ever, ever
In your incy-wincy life
Seen an incy-wincy spider
With his incy-wincy wife?

No, I've never, never, never
In my incy-wincy life
Seen an incy-wincy spider
With his incy-wincy wife.

Have you ever, ever, ever
In your diddle-diddle life
Seen a cat and a fiddle
With his diddle-diddle wife?

No, I've never, never, never
In my diddle-diddle life
Seen a cat and a fiddle
With his diddle-diddle wife.

Have you ever, ever, ever
In your goosey gander life
Seen a goosey gander wander
With his goosey gander wife?

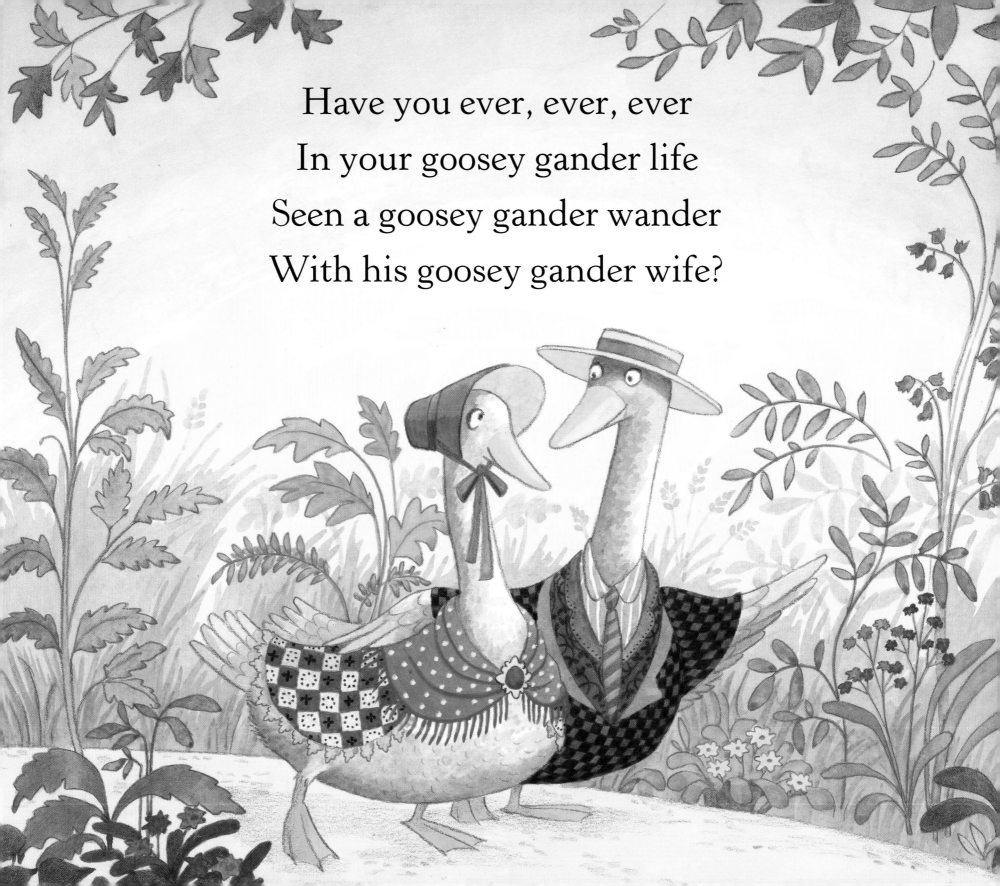

No, I've never, never, never
In my goosey gander life
Seen a goosey gander wander
With his goosey gander wife.

Have you ever, ever, ever
In your Bonny Bobby life
Seen a Bonny Bobby Shaftoe
With his Bonny Bobby wife?

No, I've never, never, never
In my Bonny Bobby life
Seen a Bonny Bobby Shaftoe
With his Bonny Bobby wife.

Have you ever, ever, ever
In your Punchinello life
Seen a Punchinello bellow
At his Punchinello wife?

No, I've never, never, never
In my Punchinello life
Seen a Punchinello bellow
At his Punchinello wife.

Have you ever, ever, ever

In your four and twenty lives

Seen four and twenty blackbirds

With their four and twenty wives?

No, I've never, never, never
In my four and twenty lives
Seen four and twenty blackbirds
With their four and twenty wives.

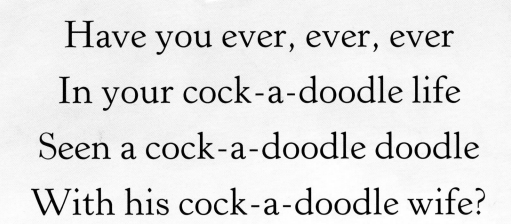

Have you ever, ever, ever
In your cock-a-doodle life
Seen a cock-a-doodle doodle
With his cock-a-doodle wife?

With a whim wham wobble ho!

No, I've never, never, never
In my cock-a-doodle life
Seen a cock-a-doodle doodle
With his cock-a-doodle wife.

No!

Have you ever, ever, ever
In your pickled pepper life
Seen a Peter Piper pick
A pickled pepper for his wife?

No, I've never, never, never
In my pickled pepper life
Seen a Peter Piper pick
A pickled pepper for his wife.

Have you ever, ever, ever
In your doodle-dandy life
Seen a Yankee doodle dandy
With his Yankee doodle wife?

No, I've never, never, never
In my doodle-dandy life
Seen a Yankee doodle dandy
With his Yankee doodle wife.

Well I never, never, never!

They live right behind this door.

I've told you of a few

But there are many, many more…

Let me introduce –
the friends of **Mother Goose!**

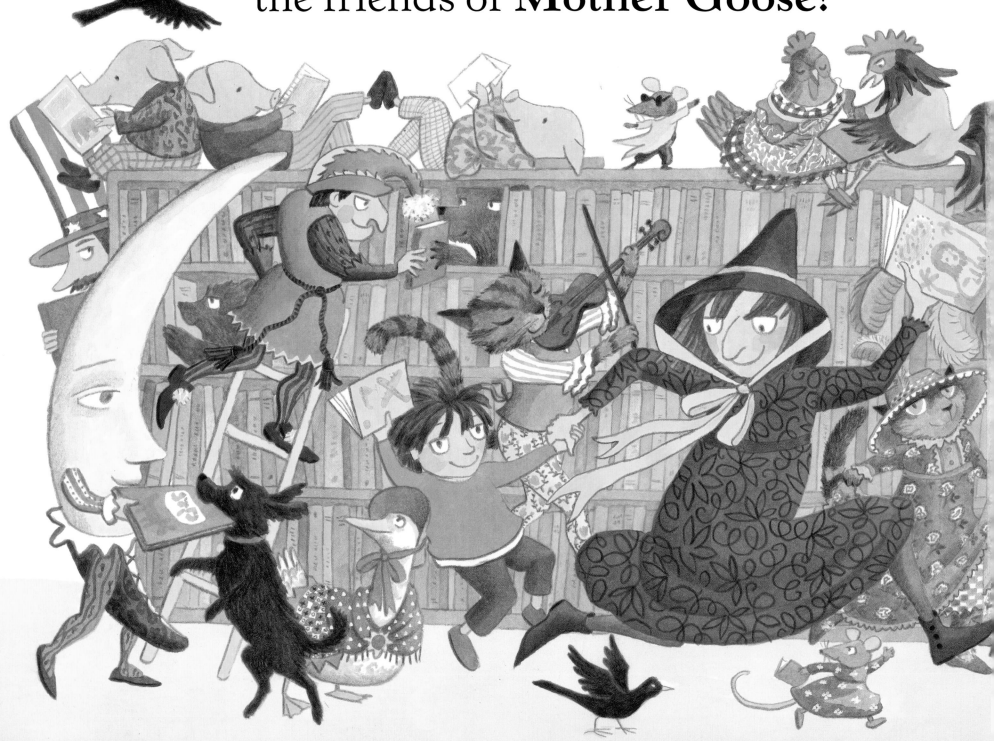

Now – have you ever, ever, ever…

THE END